Dear Reader,

I am proud to partner with Kohl's Cares and introduce young readers to Penguin and Bear. Each book features a universal theme that tugs at our hearts— such as losing and finding a favorite stuffed animal, feeling safe on a stormy night, making new (and sometimes unexpected!) friends on vacation, and the wonder of learning about new things. My hope is that when you share these books with the children in your life, they will feel as if they've just been given a warm hug and be inspired to discover more about the world around them.

I am passionate about childhood literacy and learning, and I am thrilled that Kohl's shares in this passion. Thank you for supporting Kohl's Cares and a lifelong love of reading for children everywhere!

Your friend,

Salina Yoon

For Nicole and Jason—
love will keep you safe from the storm

First published in the United States of America in January 2015
by Bloomsbury Children's Books
www.bloomsbury.com

Bloomsbury is a registered trademark of Bloomsbury Publishing Plc

For information about permission to reproduce selections from this book, write to
Permissions, Bloomsbury Children's Books, 1385 Broadway, New York, New York 10018
Bloomsbury books may be purchased for business or promotional use. For information on bulk purchases
please contact Macmillan Corporate and Premium Sales Department at specialmarkets@macmillan.com

Library of Congress Cataloging-in-Publication Data
Yoon, Salina, author, illustrator.
Stormy night / by Salina Yoon.
pages   cm
Summary: Bear is frightened by a storm, but singing to his toy Floppy and being with his parents helps comfort
him until the storm goes to sleep, and so does he.
ISBN 978-0-8027-3780-9 (hardcover)
ISBN 978-0-8027-3807-3 (e-book) • ISBN 978-0-8027-3806-6 (e-PDF)
[1. Storms—Fiction. 2. Fear—Fiction. 3. Family life—Fiction. 4. Bedtime—Fiction. 5. Bears—Fiction.] I. Title.
PZ7.Y817Sto 2015   [E]—dc23   2014012196

ISBN 978-1-68119-169-0 (Kohl's)

Art created digitally using Adobe Photoshop • Typeset in Triplex Sans • Book design by Nicole Gastonguay
Printed in China by RR Donnelley Asia, Dongguan City, Guangdong
1 3 5 7 9 10 8 6 4 2

Kohl's
Style: 1681191695
Factory Number: 123386
2/16–3/16

This special edition was printed for Kohl's Department Stores, Inc.
(for distribution on behalf of Kohl's Cares, LLC, its wholly owned subsidiary)
by Bloomsbury Children's Books.

STORMY NIGHT

Salina Yoon

BLOOMSBURY

NEW YORK LONDON OXFORD NEW DELHI SYDNEY

One stormy night,
Bear couldn't sleep.

The wind was whirring, the
trees were crackling, and the rain
was pounding against the windows.

"Don't worry," said Bear.
"I'll hold you tight. I'll keep you warm.
My love will keep you safe from the storm,"

he sang to his bunny, Floppy.

Bear felt better.

But when a thundering sound rumbled through the forest, it startled Bear.

He sang his song again.

Mama came in to check on Bear. "May I stay with you tonight? I am so frightened by the storm!"

Bear was glad to see Mama.

He kissed Mama's nose to comfort her. Mama smiled.

Bear felt better.

Then Papa came in to check
on Bear. "Is there room for me?
The storm is so loud tonight!"

Bear was glad to see Papa.
He tickled Papa's ear to comfort him.

Papa laughed! And Bear felt better.

"But what will make Floppy feel better?" thought Bear. "I know!"

"A book!"

"This is a bear-y good book!"

Bear almost forgot about the storm until . . .

A loud, crashing sound of thunder roared through the forest.

Bear shut his eyes tight.

Mama kissed his nose,

and Papa tickled his ear.

Mama sang to Bear just like
she did when he was a little cub.

"We'll hold you tight. We'll keep you warm.
Our love will keep you safe from the storm."
Bear felt better.

Bear yawned a sleepy yawn, and then it was quiet. "What happened to the storm?"

"Even storms need their sleep!" said Papa.

And so do bears!